This
# Harry
book belongs to

..................................

SCELIDOSAURUS

(ske-LI-doh-SAW-rus)

TYRANNOSAURUS

(tie-RAN-oh-SAW-rus)

TRICERATOPS

(try-SER-a-tops)

STEGOSAURUS

(STEG-oh-SAW-rus)

APATOSAURUS

(a-PAT-oh-SAW-rus)

ANCHISAURUS

(AN-ki-SAW-rus)

# SCELIDOSAURUS

(ske-LI-doh-SAW-rus)

# TYRANNOSAURUS

(tie-RAN-oh-SAW-rus)

# TRICERATOPS

(try-SER-a-tops)

# STEGOSAURUS

(STEG-oh-SAW-rus)

# APATOSAURUS

(a-PAT-oh-SAW-rus)

# ANCHISAURUS

(AN-ki-SAW-rus)

For Frank Ritter who's a big Harry fan – *I.W.*

For Rhian – *A.R.*

PUFFIN BOOKS

Published by the Penguin Group: London, New York, Australia, Canada, India, Ireland, New Zealand and South Africa
Penguin Books Ltd, Registered Offices: 80 Strand, London WC2R 0RL, England

puffinbooks.com

First published 2003
Published in this edition 2008

3 5 7 9 10 8 6 4 2

Made and printed in China
ISBN: 978-1-856-13224-4

# Harry and the Dinosaurs make a Christmas Wish

## Ian Whybrow and Adrian Reynolds

PUFFIN

It was always fun to visit Mr Oakley's farm. One time, he had some ducklings keeping warm in a box by the stove. Harry took the bucketful of dinosaurs to see.

Mr Oakley showed them one little duckling just
coming out of its shell.

Harry even held the duckling in his hands.
"Raaah! Ask him, Harry!" said the dinosaurs.
"Ask Mr Oakley for a duckling to keep."
Mr Oakley said better not. They only had room
for chickens over at Harry's house.

Mr Oakley let Harry and the dinosaurs ride home in his trailer, but they were still upset.

"Shame," said Triceratops.

"Raaah!" said Tyrannosaurus. "We want a duckling!"

"Oh I *wish* we could have one!" said Harry.

It was a big wish, but it didn't work.

Maybe it was the wrong time for wishing.

At last, one cold day in the winter, the right time came.

Nan said, "Harry, will you and the dinosaurs help me stir up the Christmas pudding mixture?"

They all had a good stir and a lick – and then they closed their eyes and they made a *special* wish, a Christmas wish!

Harry wrote down his wish in a letter to Santa.
"What did you wish for?" asked Mum.
"A duckling!" said Harry and the dinosaurs.

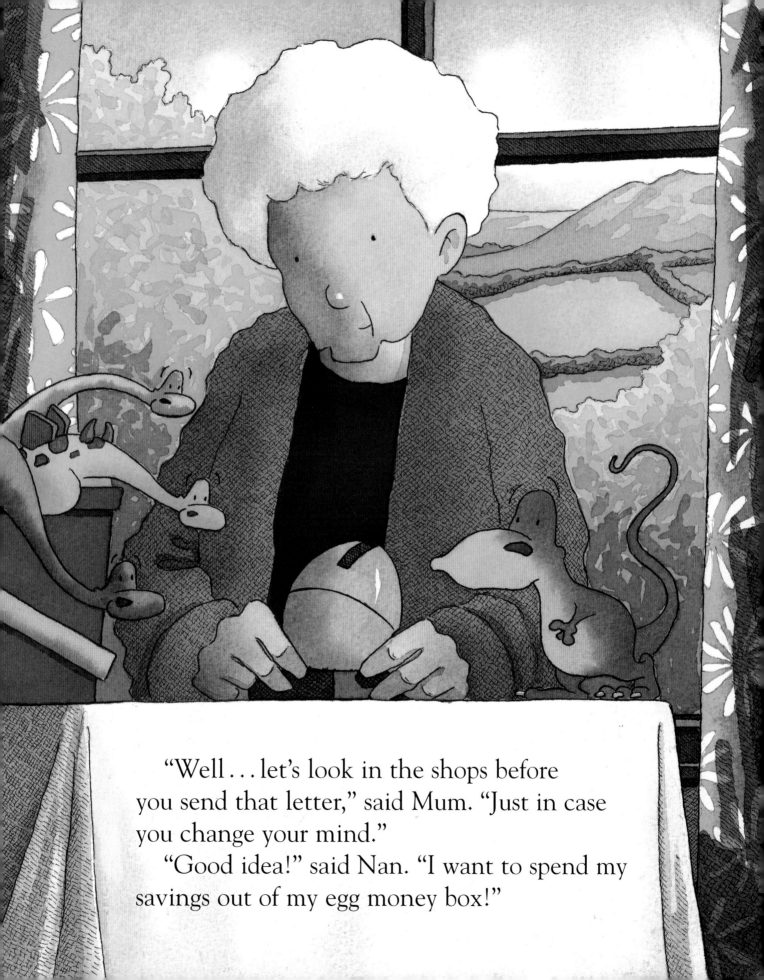

"Well...let's look in the shops before you send that letter," said Mum. "Just in case you change your mind."

"Good idea!" said Nan. "I want to spend my savings out of my egg money box!"

They all went on the bus to see the lights and the Christmas displays in the big stores.
    Harry found just the right book about dinosaurs in the bookshop.

And there was plenty Harry liked in the toyshop!
So he thought of lots more things to put in his letter.

"But don't forget to say about our duckling, Harry,"
whispered the dinosaurs.

On Christmas Eve, Nan helped Harry to hang up his stocking.

"Dinosaurs don't like presents in stockings," said Harry. "They want their present in an egg."

"I see," said Nan, "then we'll leave out my money box, shall we?"

Sam said it was stupid putting out an egg.
Eggs were for Easter, not for Christmas.
That was why Harry and the dinosaurs made
RAAAH-noises all through her favourite programme.

Nan took Harry to his room to settle down.

"I've been bad to Sam, haven't I," sighed Harry. "Now I won't get my Christmas wishes."

Nan said not to get upset. Christmas wishes were special, and if you were really sorry, Santa would understand.

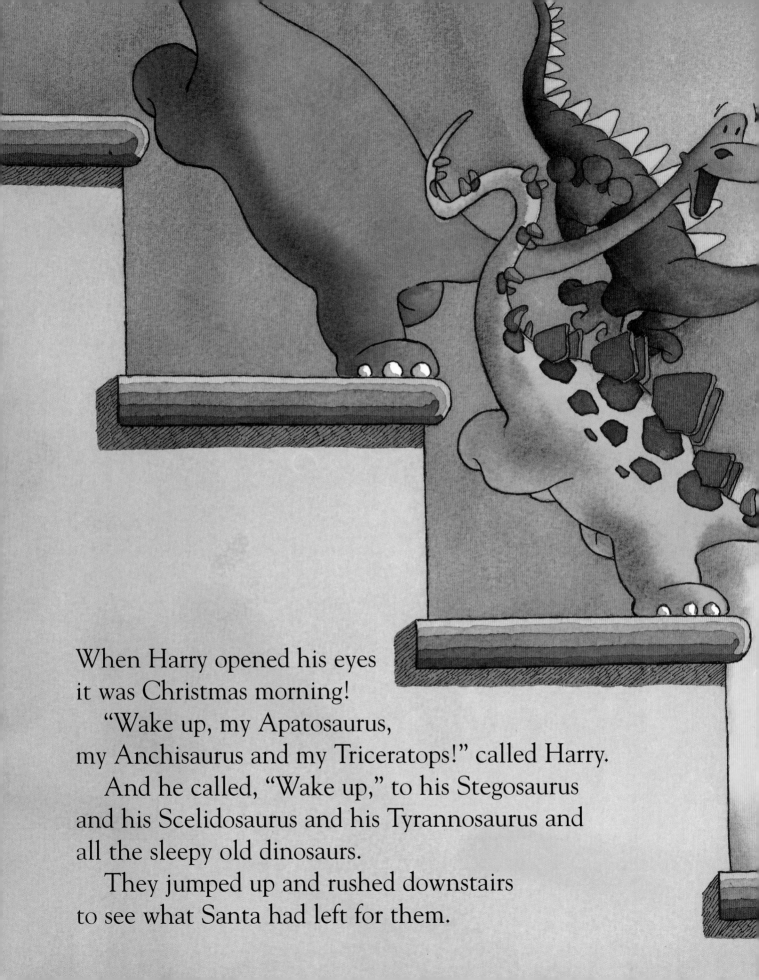

When Harry opened his eyes
it was Christmas morning!
   "Wake up, my Apatosaurus,
my Anchisaurus and my Triceratops!" called Harry.
   And he called, "Wake up," to his Stegosaurus
and his Scelidosaurus and his Tyrannosaurus and
all the sleepy old dinosaurs.
   They jumped up and rushed downstairs
to see what Santa had left for them.

Harry unwrapped all his presents.
"Just what I wanted!" he shouted every time.
   "What a shame," sighed the dinosaurs.
"Santa didn't bring us a duckling."
   "Wait!" said Harry. "You haven't opened your egg yet!"
   So all the dinosaurs closed their eyes, gave the egg a
warm-up and made a Christmas wish.
And guess what popped out . . .

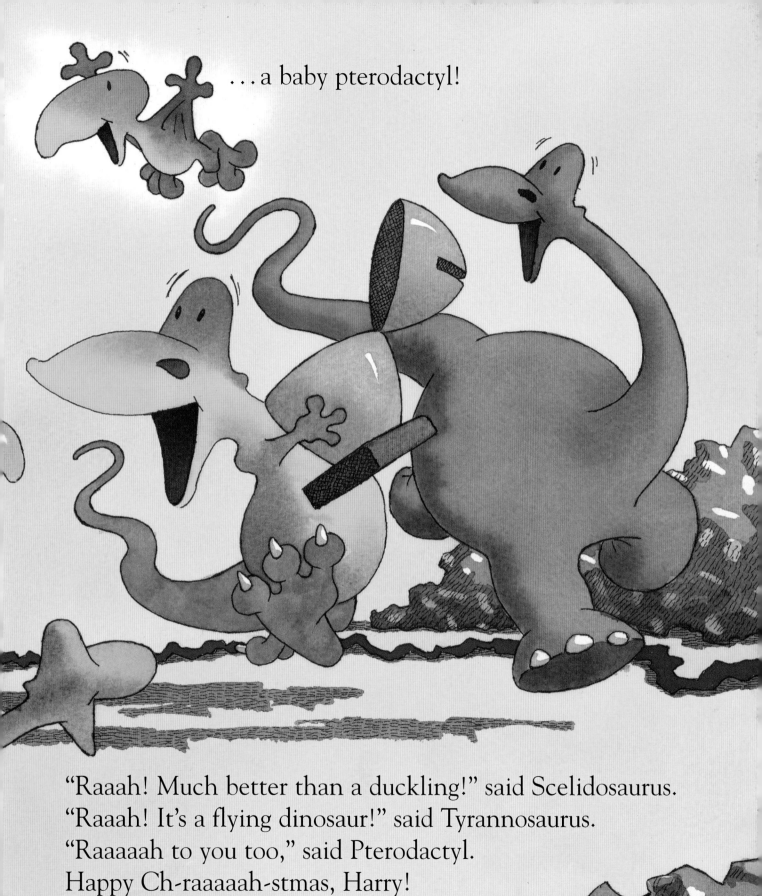

. . . a baby pterodactyl!

"Raaah! Much better than a duckling!" said Scelidosaurus.
"Raaah! It's a flying dinosaur!" said Tyrannosaurus.
"Raaaaah to you too," said Pterodactyl.
Happy Ch-raaaaah-stmas, Harry!

## SCELIDOSAURUS

(ske-LI-doh-SAW-rus)

## TYRANNOSAURUS

(tie-RAN-oh-SAW-rus)

## TRICERATOPS

(try-SER-a-tops)

## PTERODACTYL

(TER-oh-DAC-til)

## STEGOSAURUS

(STEG-oh-SAW-rus)

## APATOSAURUS

(a-PAT-oh-SAW-rus)

## ANCHISAURUS

(AN-ki-SAW-rus)

SCELIDOSAURUS

(ske-LI-doh-SAW-rus)

TYRANNOSAURUS

(tie-RAN-oh-SAW-rus)

TRICERATOPS

(try-SER-a-tops)

STEGOSAURUS

(STEG-oh-SAW-rus)

PTERODACTYL

(TER-oh-DAC-til)

APATOSAURUS

(a-PAT-oh-SAW-rus)

ANCHISAURUS

(AN-ki-SAW-rus)